XXXIX.
XL.
XLI.
XLII.
XLIII.
XLIV.
XLV.
XLVI.
XLVII.
XLVIII.
XLIX.
L.
LI.
LII.
LIII.
LIV.
LV.
LVI.
LVII.
LVIII.
LIX.
LX.
LXI.
LXII.
LXIII.
LXIV.
LXV.
LXVI.
LXVII.
LXVIII.
LXIX.
LXX.
LXXI.
LXXII.
LXXIII.
LXXIV.
LXXV.
LXXVI.
LXXVII.
LXXVIII.
LXXIX.
LXXX.
LXXXI.
LXXXII.
Carolyn Clive – A Concise Bibliography

I.

I Watch's the heav'ns above me, and a star
   Appear'd before my meditative eyes;
I mark'd the solitary beam afar
   Pursue its journey in th' eternal skies.
Calm from its distant glory, came the rays
Through all of space between us, on my gaze;
No other signs of those who dwelt therein
Fell on my sense, except that beam serene;
And fancy, soothed beneath the streaming light,
   Pursued the orb along its high career,
And deem'd it some new world, all fresh and bright
   With its ten thousand hopes, and not one fear.

II.

There did I land, upborne on wondrous wing,
   On whose strong pinion the freed spirit flies;
And mark'd around in many a beauteous thing,
   How, like our earth, it might be paradise.
Serene and sweet the lovely landscape lay
Outstretch'd beneath a summer's glancing ray;
And from blue skies a fost'ring sun like ours,
Swell'd in the fruits, and glitter'd in the flow'rs.
Above, the silent mountains stood on high,
Their outline graved distinct along the sky;
And forests stretch'd their undulating wreath,
Above the vales that smiling slept beneath;
While far away, the breath of fresh perfume
   Pass'd on the breeze which rose from western caves,
And o'er the glow of summer's form and bloom,
   Calm ocean's voice came up from slowly moving waves.

III.

Man's mind, if turned harmonious to the scene,
   Might here have felt its glory all expand;
Reason, and joy, and feeling, would have been
   Call'd forth and echo'd in that lovely land.
Here dwelt that spell upon the mountain's brow,
Which calls to life the bosom's generous glow;
Here smiled that spirit on the mirror lake,
From which our feelings holy calmness take;
And breeze, and bloom, and change of night and day,
   Held commune with the soul's more noble part;

I Watched the Heavens by Caroline Clive

Caroline Meysey-Wigley was born on June 24th 1801 in Brompton Grove, London, the daughter of Edmund Meysey-Wigley, Esq., of Shakenhurst, Worcestershire, M.P. for Worcester, and his wife, Anna Maria Meysey.

A severe illness contracted when she was three left her with several after-effects chief amongst them was lameness.

During her lifetime she became a respected and well-regarded poet and author. All of her works were published anonymously, using the pen name, "V".

In 1840, her 'IX Poems' appeared in a small duodecimo, which Hartley Coleridge reviewed in the September edition of the Quarterly Review:—

"We suppose V stands for Victoria, and really she queens it among our fair friends. Perhaps V will think it a questionable compliment, if we say, like the late Baron Graham to Lady —, in the Assize Court at Exeter, 'We beg your ladyship's pardon, but we took you for a man.' Indeed, these few pages are distinguished by a sad Lucretian tone, such as very seldom comes from a woman's lyre. But V is a woman, and no ordinary woman certainly; though, whether spinster, wife, or widow, we have not been informed. The stanzas printed by us are, in our judgment, worthy of any one of our greatest poets in his happiest moments."

It was very fine praise indeed and was only one of many.

Later that year on November 10th, she married the Reverend Archer Clive. The union would produce a son (1842) and a daughter (1843).

Caroline continued to write and the following year, 1841, published a second edition of 'IX Poems' which was followed by 'I Watched the Heavens' (1842); 'The Queen's Ball' (1847); 'Valley of the Rea' (1851); and 'The Morlas' (1853). She now also began to add novels to her publications beginning with one from the popular sensational genre: 'Paul Ferroll: A Tale' (1855). It was hugely successful.

In literary terms, aside from her poems, her reputation is most burnished by 'Paul Ferroll' and its sequel, 'Why Paul Ferroll Killed his Wife'. The first is generally accepted to be the most superior of all her works and passed into several editions and translations. It was only with the fourth edition that the concluding chapter, which brought the story down to the death of Paul Ferroll, was added. 'V' was now a respected and popular novelist to go with her glowing reputation as a poet.

'Paul Ferroll' is considered the precursor of the genre 'sensational novel' or of what may be called the novel mystery. Caroline was included in the forefront of the sensational novelists of the 19th-century, anticipating the works of Wilkie Collins, Charles Reade, Miss Braddon, and many others, writing of human nature as defined by its energies, neither diagnosing it like a physician, nor analysing it like a priest.

Caroline's health was always a delicate issue and for many years prior to her death she was a confirmed invalid.

Caroline Clive died when her dress caught fire whilst she was seated in her boudoir and among her papers on July 13th 1873, at Whitfield, Herefordshire.

Index of Contents
I WATCHED THE HEAVENS
I.
II.
III.
IV.
V.
VI.
VII.
VIII.
IX.
X.
XI.
XII.
XIII.
XIV.
XV.
XVI.
XVII.
XVIII.
XIX.
XX.
XXI.
XXII.
XXIII.
XXIV.
XXV.
XXVI.
XXVII.
XXVIII.
XXIX.
XXX.
XXXI.
XXXII.
XXXIII.
XXXIV.
XXXV.
XXXVI.
XXXVII.
XXXVIII.

And fain would lead it, on its destined way,
    All dignified the mind, all calm and good the heart.

IV.

"O Thou, whose ample page, if read aright,
    Stirs the immortal in the mortal's breast,
If here there dwell a race not fallen quite,
    They are already, or they may be bless'd;
 For thou hast lov'd this new-found Globe to dress,
And make it fit for Eden happiness.
And if its dwellers like itself be pure,
    Glory and Peace will mantle o'er their doom;
Man here might see his promised hope secure—
    This is, perchance, the shore whose ocean is the tomb."

V.

While thus I ponder'd, onward came a form,
    Unlike the dream which flatter'd Fancy's sight,
Man's shape he wore, but some internal storm
    Defaced the image, and put out its light.
His inward spirit seem'd by thoughts o'ercast
Whose shadow o'er his visage darkly pass'd,
And to his eye that lovely land was dim,
Suggesting nought of peace or joy to him—
He heard no accent in the wind, and flood,
    The landscape had no meanings for his eye,
In vain before him in their joy they stood,
    For joy's responding sources in his heart were dry.

VI.

"Being!—what art thou?" I exclaim'd, and gazed
    In wonder on his stricken form and face;
On me his haggard eyes he slowly raised,
    And paused a few short moments in his place.
I know not what of deadly pain there came
In gradual current through his shaken frame,
But while he mark'd me, old Remembrance seem'd
    To pass before him with its phantom crew,
Like one who fainting on the rock has dream'd
    Of childhood'd scenes, which crowd his thoughts anew,
Forgot through guilty years—but oh, how dear and true!

VII.

"And what art thou?" he answer'd me. "Canst thou,
    A mortal, stand still mortal on this shore?
Back, back to earth, man's happiest dream to know—
    Dream thou shalt die—Death comes to us no more!"
With that he toss'd his weary arms on high,
And look'd despairing at the sunny sky,
While cold dews rose upon his ashy brow,
    Wrung fiercely from his inward agony,
As though he felt the curse upon him now,
    The everlasting doom, the fix'd command, to be.

VIII.

"Death comes not here?" I cried; "O spirit, say,
    Why dwells then on thy face that print of pain;
This land seems one where joyful souls might stray,
    And find their home, their native heav'n again."
Darkly he answer'd—"Ay, if place could make
    That joy wherein the soul aspires to dwell;
The land, the land, perchance, such thoughts may wake—
    Ay, all around is heaven, but here within is hell."

IX.

So saying, on the ground his form he threw,
    And gnash'd the herbs around him in his woe,
Then his clench'd hand towards the skies he threw,
    And gibber'd words like hate, but short and low,
Forced through closed teeth, as though his inward pain
Sought something to accuse, and sought in vain.
At length his eyes upon my face he turn'd,
Where fire, like tomb-lamps lit by sorrow, burn'd,
And bade me forward—"Go, and see beyond,
    The fallen spirits, and the scene they suit—
God to their guidance leaves the outcast land,
    Sin works its will uncheck'd—go see its gracious fruit!"

X.

I wander'd onward, stricken with his word,
    And look'd for some new form as dread as this;
But yet no sound of voice or step was heard,

And nature smiled in her untroubled bliss.
Deep quiet vistas of green wood uprose,
And flow'rs beneath illumined their repose;
When sunbeams piercing through the quiv'ring shade,
Shot changeful brightness up the summer glade.
 At length, where hung above the flood, a tree,
   I saw a shape, sit tranquil as the scene;
And deem'd the sentence not for him, and he
    Was there rejoicing, and rejoiced by Nature's mien.

XI.

 But as I gazed, a horror o'er me came,
   Like one who enters in a gloomy place,
And there, with doubtful eyes and startled frame,
   Sees from the darkness grow a form and face.
Changed was that face, and dim the look it wore,
Yet still it was the same I knew of yore;
But, oh! how alter'd from that happier day,
When mind shone through it with its fiery ray!
Keen, joyous, then—and in those hours of earth,
   Whate'er he touch'd became a brighter thing;
E'en vice, when he would wreathe it, in his mirth,
    Grew fair beneath the flowers which o'er it he would fling.

XII.

 Stilly he sat, but on his hueless cheek
   'Twas no elysian peace that fix'd ts reign,
But brooding stillness, whose dark shadows speak
   Of reason lost in a benighted bra n.
And that quick eye, which, glittering once with wit,
Mark'd and adorn'd each form that courted it,
Now heavily was fix'd on one lone spot,
And even there beheld, but mark'd it not.
His lips had sunk asunder; and the smile
   That came like lightning seemed extinct for ever;
His slacken'd brow was blank of light the while,
    Where glow'd his genius once, as though to perish never.

XIII.

 I call'd him by his name—he did not mark;
   His fame, it seem'd forgotten in his doom;
Like the silk pennon on a sinking bark,

Or wither'd flow'rs upon a last-year's tomb.
Then from my memory, words of his I brought,
Wherein he once had cloth'd a splendid thought,
And he look'd up as though the pausing dart
Which press'd before, now enter'd in his heart.
"Gone—gone!" he cried, and one expiring ray
Of mind return'd, to shew how thick the night,
Then vanish'd in the gath'ring clouds away,
Like storms dispersed a moment ere they quench the light.

XIV.

"Art thou so fallen?" I exclaim'd—"What, thou?
Earth-worshipp'd man, our glory, and our grace,—
Where is the wreath which twines thy statue's brow?
Where is th' Elysium which we deem'd thy place?"
"Thou speakest language of a world gone by,"
Slowly he answered—"lowest, last am I."
And while he spoke, I thought of time behind,
When once beside a dotard's seat he stood,
Mocking the dull face, in his pride of mind—
Then, how unlike his own! how near his present mood!

XV.

"Yet, once," I answer'd, "words were not so fleet,
But thou hadst caught their sense before 'twas said;
Things dark to others thou wouldst half-way meet,
And turn them all to daylight 'mid the shade."
"Am I as then?" he answer'd. "Then I was
Happy." He spoke, and dismal was the pause;
Then round he gazed on the delicious land—
But to his eyes, alas! 'twas dull and void—
And murmur'd, stretching forth each empty hand,
"I feel existence only, which I once enjoy'd."

XVI.

"This is thy penance, then," I cried; but he,
In such dull accents as before, replied—
"Ay, call it penance, if such name may be
To things by nature join'd in one, applied.
Ay, penance, for I might have been as high
As Joy can lead a dweller of the sky,
If passions brought from earth had not decay'd

This subtle frame, for Joy and Virtue made;
 But they have bow'd and rent it, till behold
   The hopeless, helpless wretch that I am grown;
Earth was the place to check them or unfold —
   Cruel as true thy word, my penance is my own."

XVII.

Pitying I heard; but while mine ear I bent,
   Arose a cry that spoke the extreme of ill,
Prolong'd by passion when the breath was spent,
   Renew'd again ere one might say 'tis still.
And, oh, what mingled dread was surging thence!
Fear, fury's yell, and agony intense;
And of some deed, some sight,—the story told,
I dared not think on, yet must fain behold;
And, rushing headlong toward the sounding place,
   Through bush and brake I strove to force my way,
As one who would behold a murder'd face
   Tears off the pall in haste, too fearful to delay.

XVIII.

And there—oh Heaven! oh Heaven!—that fearful sight!
   Man, what a fiend, when turned to ill, art Thou!
What aspects human eyes and thoughts to blight,
Tortured and torturer, met my glances now!
For both uprose before me—both, too, wore
Man's form, and yet a human form no more;
But shaped by inner thoughts, till they were grown
Things that the mortal eye ne'er look'd upon.
One fasten'd to a stake was writing there,
   With hell's own aspect on his form and face,
And round, the inflictors stood, on whom Despair
   Was written with another, but an equal trace.

XIX.

Where are the burning words that paint the pains
   By spirits on their fellow-spirits wrought?
Things which earth's tyrant racks and dungeon chains
   But shadow forth, as speech interprets thought.
Not human pain was there, for that can slay,
And from the man divide the suffering clay;
But pangs that press'd on naked mind their smart,

And lived with life in each immortal part;
Such as inflame on earth, the torturer's will—
   The eager will which leaves his pow'r behind;
The will, the power, in hell are present still,
    But that wherewith, whereon, they work is Mind.

XX.

In vain I strive to pain the how—the why;
   Earth has no words to fix th' unearthly thing—
The outer signs they wrung from Misery,
   The tone, the look, the act, are all I sing;
And, oh! how howl'd upon the ethers sleep
The load of shrieks from that unceasing lip;
How flash'd the light that elsewhere slept serene,
In horrid lightning from that frantic mien!
Passion's extremest utterance, mingled wild
   With pain, a load of wrong and rage to wreak;
At times, the inflicting host his voice reviled
   In words which might have ruin'd worlds to speak—
At times himself he wail'd in that blaspheming shriek.

XXI.

Around, not less demoniac, shew'd the crew,
   Tossing and wild, like some tempestuous wave;
Each with fresh torture heap'd his pain anew,
   And bitter speech increased the pang they gave.
Unknown to them satiety of pain—
Unknown Remorse, which, waking not in vain
On earth, amid her worst and fiercest band,
Holds from the last excess the shrinking hand;
But these no sympathizing feelings knew,
   By which man makes the cause of man his own;
No saving influence the hand withdrew,
   Where all alike had pow'r, and pity dwelt with none.

XXII.

All who from him had suffer'd wrong were there,
   Whose souls, debased, for vengeance thirsted still;
All he compell'd on earth his yoke to bear,
   By fortune slaves, but tyrants by their will.
Nor were earth's debts alone to be defray'd—
   He lived in hell the tyrant he had died;

And spirits here the recent wrong repaid
    With eager haste upon his conquer'd head.
"Remember earth—remember hell!" they said;
    "This, for the long pass'd, long remember'd wrong;
And this, for yesterday's still burning deed,
    For which we thank our fate thou hast not waited long."

XXIII.

With wild demoniac laugh they urged their glee,
    For frighted look'd they with their own success,
Like one who, murd'ring his worst enemy,
    Grows mad with his loud cry and struggling face.
And he, their victim, shriek'd, till all among
The vales and hills one voice of torment rung;
And ghastly shapes came forth in living swarms,
Peopling the sunny rocks with dismal forms,
And mark'd the madd'ning scene, till some flung high
Their tossing arms, and join'd the frantic cry,
And some approach'd with staring eyes, as though
To harden hearts, not yet quite hard to woe;
And some affrighted, fled with speed, that fain
    Would find a refuge 'gainst the direful crew;
And crazed with fear, came full in sight again,
    Then strain'd their weary limbs, and, shrieking, fled anew.

XXIV.

I heard—I saw the deepening horror roll,
    Increasing ever as the moments fled;
Till like some lengthen'd storm it mazed the soul,
    And, like a mist, was fear around them spread.
I saw not individual crime or woe,
A troubled sea, it raged and burst below,
Till, like the taper shining on the shore,
Which shews the storm-toss'd bark its port once more,
A form across the raving people press'd,
Whose heart one human feeling still possess'd:
I saw him stoop and loose the wretches' chain,
    And they, it may be, tired, allow'd the deed—
"We meet as erst on earth," he said; "Again,
    Old comrade, will I aid thy hour of need."

XXV.

Released, he fled at once—yet turn'd to shout
    A yell of rage that sank to agony;
And from their gather'd ranks a cry rang out
    Of mockery, bitter as the fiends' could be.
But faster fled he—Fear was stronger then
    Than even Vengeance, hot in every vein;
And with a watchful eye, I turn'd to mark
    How, refuge 'gainst his fellow-kind to gain,
He sought the waving forest cool and dark,
    While o'er him bent the tree alleviating his pain.

XXVI.

Intent to bring relief, more near I drew;
    But, starting, fearful, when my words began,
He dragg'd his limbs o'er earth in flight anew,
    Like some crush'd serpent at the sight of man.
In vain I sought to re-assure his dread—
In vain to quench it by some kindly deed—
Wing'd by his fear, his quiv'ring frame he sped,
And Fear became more fearful as he fled;
Till 'neath the roots of an o'erhanging tree,
    Which from the bank a little space was set,
Groaning, he crawl'd, and turn'd to gaze on me,
    Coil'd in his narrow nook, and glaring Fear and Hate.

XXVII.

I left him, hopelessly, and wandered on,
All doleful sounds, all dreary sights among,
And e'en where Heaven's light best and brightest shone,
Methought the night of mind most darkly hung.
Some sat in the sun's rays, and mark'd it rise
Along its daily pathway of the skies,
With vacant eye, which knew to them 'twould be
The same one hour through all eternity.
Some built such fabrics as on earth express
    Man's pomp or pride, and when aloft they grew,
Smote them to dust again for weariness,
    And then for weariness began their work anew.

XXVIII.

There toil'd in the vain labour many an one,
    Whose wishes linger'd in the world behind,

Coil'd round the things and creatures that were gone—
　　The haunting phantoms of his cumber'd mind.
There stood the man, whose transitory pleasure
Had been Earth's glittering joys, or golden treasure;
And who revived, amid a world destroy'd,
To live when all was dead that he enjoy'd.
　Amazed with objects which had met his eye
　　When re-awaking, he arose from death;
He turn'd to look for earth, and saw it lie
　　Expiring in its flames, with all he loved beneath.

XXIX.

　Not far apart, the Conqueror, who had fought
　　To make himself a name, stood nameless by;
One spot of earth had been the prize he sought,
　　Whose whole orb now had faded from the sky;
And round thro' that Existence infinite—
He, restless, turn'd his ever-wand'ring sight,
Gazing through worlds which shone with countless flame,
For that within whose bound he left his fame;
But none that Fame remember'd, and he grew
　　A vacant wand'rer, past remembrance riven;
Save when some giber of the demon crew
　　Mock'd at the homage he on earth had given.

XXX.

　Beyond these, some had tried to bring anew
　　Time's pleasures into vast eternity;
The sound of music round the circle flew,
　　And forms went flitting to its melody.
But seem'd it, as if one who watch'd the bed
Where all he loved the best, in death was laid,
Should rise, and in the dead one's presence play
The idle games that pleased him yesterday.
For strange the eyes I mark'd among the group,
　　And haggard pale the cheeks, and slack the mien,
While to these sports unconscious did they stoop,
　　Pond'ring far other thoughts meantime within.

XXXI.

And one by one they stopp'd, as though the heart
　　Fail'd at the endless echo of the strain;

Gazed in each other's face and turn'd apart,
  Or sat them down, as ne'er to rise again.
And smile or laugh was not; for they who yet
Moved to the music did it as a debt,
  And seem'd to feel it was a pain to be,
The pain of vacant immortality;
Till all, at last, were still; and then the sound
  Of the gay, grievous strain, was heard the more,
Recurring still with its perpetual round,
  Dead language of Delight, whose life was o'er.

XXXII.

Methought that there were none more lost to God
  Than souls on former pleasures so employ'd,
Who, with all Heaven appointed their abode,
  Clung to the shadows of a world destroy'd.
And when I saw Mind's vast capacity
Wheel lagging round a little point, and be
A burden to itself from day to day,
  I bow'd lamenting, o'er their former pride,
As when the Magian swept a world away,
  Over its ruin'd beauty, spirits sigh'd.

XXXIII.

Soul-struck, I turn'd away; and from the throng
  Went musing on, while still the weary strain
Came with its joyless melody along,
  Repeating in my ear its antic pain.
And some I saw, who cast them down, and laid,
Hearing the sound, in their clench'd hand, their head,
As though they could not brook that earthly voice,
Which once they answered when it said, Rejoice.
And some, in quicker ecstasy of woe,
  Cried out aloud, and toss'd them at the tone,
As though life's pain again were running through
  A form by Torture almost turn'd to stone.

XXXIV.

But now I left behind those sounds of wail,
  And follow'd where grey rocks on either side
Rose up aloft above a narrow vale,
  And in the sun's light bathed their brows of pride.

But all below was shadow'd, and so still,
I heard the long grass move upon the hill.
 Here hell was silent, and it seem'd almost
    The inward fire might lave itself to rest,
If one could stand alone, of that wild host,
    Mid the grave calmness of the mountain's breast.
And to them, truly, it had seem'd a place
    Where Quiet still might find one sacred spot;
For, as I turn'd a vast rock's jutting base—
    A scene before me lay which I have not forgot.

XXXV.

Tall Cypress trees had rear'd themselves on high,
    About a mountain's foot that clos'd the view;
And resting in its bed, a lake lay by,
    Repeating point and line, precise and true.
No breeze disturb'd it in its deep serene;
No moving thing reflected life therein;
A changeless copy of the scene it lent,
    Which rose above it motionless; its face
In the mysterious mirror downward bent,
    Fix'd, yet unreal, like the forms in Memory's glass.

XXXVI.

And there, between the water and the trees,
    The spirits had erected tombs, like those
Which Earth in every tranquil churchyard sees,
    Yielding to sad and gay the same repose.
To me, too, seem'd they quiet; for my mind
Had with such outer, inner calm combin'd;
And I believed that in this place of rest,
    The sentence of the spirit was unbound;
And gazed upon each hillock's awful breast,
    Where mind, annihilation's peace had found.

XXXVII.

But while I gazed, from the vault's hollow cave
    Crawl'd shapes, still animate with living breath,
As comes the unquiet worm from out the grave,
    Where, living, dwells he in the house of death;
Clothed in the garments of the dead were they,
The shroud and cerement of corrupting clay;

And from our own earth's vault and sepulchre,
Whatever told of death they copied there.
 With vain desire they long'd aside to fling
   Their new-born weight of immortality,
And yearning t'ward earth's last and lowest thing,
   Made all their aim and purpose, not to be.

XXXVIII.

 But there they sat on the grave's edge, and sigh'd,
   And saw the scene around with sleepless eye,
That roved unquiet o'er the breathless tide,
   Or wander'd upward through the sunny sky;
Then turn'd again toward the narrow tomb,
Till grew another hope from out the gloom;
And rising, with the death-clothes round them, press'd
The heavy foldings, corpse-like, on their breast;
And once again descending, laid them there,
Extended still, and straight upon the bier.
But rest they could not; and the quiv'ring lid
   Struggled and open'd from the eye once more;
And, forc'd again to leave death's mimic bed,
   They rose, and left the grave all deathless as before.

XXXIX.

One, more than all, hung clingingly on death,
   And longest lay in copy of his form;
Nor seem'd to quit the shadowy place beneath,
   Till driven to motion by his bosom's storm.
Then, as an exile meets a stranger's land,
He turn'd to life, from whose detested strand
He gazed upon the tomb with such despair,
   Such yearning wishes in his look confess'd,
As though he said, "My spirit's home is there—
   My country! wherefore dost thou spurn me from thy breast?"

XL.

Then, on a stone he sat him down, beside
   The water, where it join'd the margin sand;
And on the shore, left arid by the tide,
   He shaped out letters with a slender wand.
I drew toward him, asking why he mourn'd?
And he his wither'd face upon me turn'd,

And answer'd, (pointing to the sand below,
With sorrow's languid hand,) "There lies my woe."
I look'd, and saw the many lines he made,
   Varied in every form, yet still the same;
For there his thoughts their lone impression laid,
    And in a thousand characters had traced one name.

XLI.

"Tharia" and "Tharia," written on the ground,
   Met him where'er below he turn'd his sight;
To him, perchance, the name was magic-bound,
   And told a form all love, an eye all light.
But nought I saw, except the writer's hand
That stamp'd a female name upon the sand;
And ask'd him whom and what those letters brought,
   With faithful symbol, back on memory?
And where was pass'd the being of his thought,
   That thus he mourn'd her in eternity?

XLII.

"No more with me!" he said; "the grave received
   That form from out my arms, whose shade will be
With life's whole texture ever interweaved,
   Though life now spreads to immortality.
Here lies her image, like the corpse of one
From whom the friend, the soul, the self is gone;
A lamp, in a deserted house, that burns,
Lit by a hand that never more returns.
That face of placid quiet, is not her's
   Whom every change of mine erewhile could move;
That eye no longer at my presence stirs,
   Which was the mirror to my joy, my grief, my love."

XLIII.

"How parted ye?" I ask'd; "What fate severe
   Forbade to both one common destiny?
Alas! if thou aspiredst not with her,
   How 'scap'd the thing belov'd, to sink with thee?"
"No, no!" he answer'd; "she with purer eyes,
Look'd through earth's gladness to the gladder skies;
A bird, that resting in a mid-way land,
Loves that, but better loves the home beyond!

Gladly she went; although her eyes' last ray
   Linger'd, and call'd me through the shadows dim;
But from myself I cast that hope away,
   Forgetting God in grief, and losing all with him.

XLIV.

I thought of her alone on earth; of her
   Alone, beyond the bounds of earth and time;
All other objects were forgot that stir
   The spirit to a strife for scenes sublime.
Earth was a desert, death was her abode—
I thought not how the life beyond it glow'd;
Few flitting years were doom'd our hearts to sever—
But I have changed the parting to For Ever.
For fondly to the grave I turn'd, and there
   Believed was meeting, and my soul's relief;
Or hoped, at least, to die to my despair,
   And did the murmurer's act, the suicide of grief.

XLV.

"But oh, we met not!—'tis not death that brings
   The hearts together whom his hands divide;
Beyond his empire rose immortal things,
   Which, madman-like, I laid my thoughts aside;
Truth, Glory, Goodness, and the Spirit's strength,
Wrought out from all earth's trial-woes, at length,
Alone, are dwellers of that happier clime,
Where she rejoices in her fate sublime;
I saw her, and the grief which o'er her threw,
Beholding what I was, its mortal hue,
Clear'd cloud-like from her face, as, new and bright,
Heaven shed on her accepted soul its light.
And then for ever parted, e'en in thought,
   She entered with no backward look, her rest,
Unseen her place, my place by her unsought,
   We never meet again; and she by that is bless'd."

XLVI.

"Had she been like thee, thou wert happy then?
   Together ye had dwelt, and that were bliss?"
Thus eagerly I questioned him, to win
   His answer to an anxious thought like this.

"Ay, perfect bliss!" he cried; yet while he said,
Like one by self denied, he sank his head;
And glanc'd toward a neighbouring tomb, where leant
Two figures on the uprear'd monument.
One was their Fate; one World, one ceaseless Life;
    United, earth-like, save with closer doom;
Yet worn they look'd, as with the spirit's strife,
    And chose, as emblem of their wish, a tomb.

XLVII.

Silent they sate upon the vaulted den
    Which other hands, in other days, had rear'd;
And which the first indwellers quitted, when
    The hope for which they built it, disappear'd.
Their hands were join'd, it seem'd, because, of old,
It was their wont each other's hands to fold;
Their eyes no more were t'ward each other raised,
Or conscious that fond looks upon them gazed;
But various and apart, as though the thought
Of either heart, no common centre sought.
The woman's wander'd o'er the land serene,
    Restless and seeking, and yet hopeless now;
The man's were all unconscious of the scene,
    Fix'd on one point, beneath his gather'd brow.

XLVIII.

I stood and gazed at distance, and it seem'd
    As though their deathlessness on them too weigh'd;
And love, which bright enough for earth had beam'd,
    Here a faint insufficient twilight made.
The heart, enlarged by immortality,
    Seem'd void of half that it had room to hold;
An empty palace, bare to wind and sky,
    Prepared for king-like pomp, but desert, worn, and cold.

XLIX.

I pass'd them slowly by; perusing still
    Their languid attitude and careless mien;
But did not question; for their spirit's ill
    Enough in every look and line was seen.
He mark'd me not; but she, with restless sight,
Caught on the wave my shadow o'er the light;

Then smiled so new a face to see, and took
Her hand from his, yet turn'd again to look
If stirr'd no jealous feeling at the deed,
   Or if the stranger woke no sleeping pain;
But no, he did but fold the arms she freed;
    Then sitting down she sigh'd, and sought his hand again.

L.

I also sigh'd; for she was fair and bright,
   And might have been the angel she was not;
Yet was her beauty day's decaying light,
   And faintly told of radiance half forgot.
It was the wreck of feelings warm and high,
That hallow'd once, and honour'd still, her eye;
 Feelings which, worthy to expand in heaven,
To things too mean had been too rashly given;
Like lightning, which, if aim'd aright, would be
   Life to an altar pile, to God upraised;
But wasted on the cold unkindly sea,
   Dies on the element whereon awhile it blazed.

LI.

Grieved at the fall of one so fair, I moved
   With pensive step and heavy heart away;
And forward through the place of tombs I roved,
   Where'er the path invited me to stray.
Tenantless graves and unfill'd shrouds lay round,
Adding new horror to the barren ground;
Those earthy beds had lost their tenants now,
   And wore not e'en the image of repose;
Forth in the world they had resolved to go,
   To seek, though not to hope, some refuge from their woes.

LII.

Here where most mournful, was the mournful place
   Deserted, barren, hopeless, and accurst,
 Sate scatter'd far upon the tomb-grown grass,
Some who, mid all things drear, still sought the worst;
Erewhile on earth they bow'd 'neath sorrow's storm,
Sinking to dust their unelastic form;
And if one joy from out their fate was reft,
Refused to see all comfort that was left.

E'en in the common pangs of human care
  Themselves inflamed the wound that tore their breast;
And fond of anguish, jealous of despair,
  They claim'd to be earth's mourners most oppress'd.

LIII.

In this new world, from all that soothed they turn'd,
  And e'en the straggling sunbeam shut from view;
Save where upon some barren rock it burn'd,
  Where flowers grew not, nor rose the nurt'ring dew.
They sate by arid sand, and tomb forlorn,
Dry stones by winter's current sear'd and worn,
 Where hands despairing, ere they came, had rent
Each green herb climbing o'er the monument.
For those who built them, sought a place which shew'd
  Congenial temper to a grieving mind;
But these had chosen the forlorn abode,
  To feed the sullen thoughts they fain would make or find.

LIV.

Oh me! they were so wretched! The long flow
  Of age on age had deepen'd their despair;
The shadows which began on earth to grow,
  Flung their unbounded shroud about them here.
Thick darkness darken'd more, as round them flow'd
The ceaseless youth of this unbless'd abode,
Till grief became the food whereon they fed,
  Th' essential substance of their very frame;
Their soul's one thought, their spirit's needful dread,
  Their element of life, an ever-gnawing flame.

LV.

Chill'd with their aspect, motionless and cold,
  At little distance did I sit me down,
Like him a serpent's fascinations hold,
  And fix'd my eyes upon the eyes of one.
Not by my pencil can the gloom be shewn
That o'er his awful lineaments was thrown—
Drawn lips were there, all colourless and fix'd;
Glassy, yet living eyes; their ray unmix'd
With e'en a motion, that might speak within
The heart less frozen than the icy mien.

His was the shrunken limb, all still and drear,
　　The rigid hands that held the heavy brow;
As though for years the soul had ceased to stir
　　The heart to hope, the frame to move, the thoughts to flow.

LVI.

By slow degrees accustom'd to the sight,
　　I nearer drew and touch'd with awe his hand;
Then bolder press'd it, that th' arousing might
　　Of outer things might break the spirit's band.
He stirr'd at length; his stony eyes rose slow,
And fix'd on mine their blank cold gaze of woe:
But wordless for a space, until at last
　　My boldness rais'd his spirit from its shroud,
The o'er his face a brief fierce radiance pass'd,
　　As leaps the flame once more from some consumed abode.

LVII.

"What dost thou, and what wilt thou, rude unknown?"
　　Thus spoke a voice half buried in its breast;
It seem'd the echo of a world long gone,
　　Which should have slept ere now, and been at rest.
"What has thy asking face, thy idle bloom,
To do where nature shares the spirit's gloom?
Hast thou not yet renounced the futile strife
　　Of those who think their early dreams are true?
Earth might have shewn, since thou art cursed with life,
　　That thou no more shalt cease the fatal gift to rue."

LVIII.

"Not yet," I cried, "has it been rued," for I
　　Who loved existence started at his word;
"Sad should I be to feel life's fountain dry,
　　Which healthfully my bosom's pulse has stirr'd.
Some bitter waters I have drunk therein,
And on its surface early ice-flakes seen;
Some forms, which once their dear reflection gave,
No more are imaged on the ruffled wave;
And hues I saw there, 'neath the dawning sky,
Have melted as the noon-day hour drew nigh.
Yet as they vanish, other colours rise,
　　And paint the stream whose course I love to feel,

Fresh from its waves elastic pleasure flies,
   And reason's calmer joys forth from the current steal."

LIX.

Uprose that figure as I paused, and laugh'd;
   E'en such a sound might burst from forth the dead,
And on the watcher's soul dismay engraft,
   Who kept his vigil by the sheeted bed.
Still as the corpse was every muscle fix'd,
The cheeks blank whiteness, as before, unmix'd;
That hollow laugh no human feeling spoke,
   No smile, no sparkle mingled with the sound,
And 'mid the desert silence which it broke,
   Rang the harsh voice, unnaturally round.

LX.

Rous'd at the accent, from full many a grave
   Uprais'd the spectre-forms their doleful head;
To mark what lip this troubled accent gave,
   That broke the age-kept silence of their bed.
Their sunken eyes gleam'd out upon the day,
Like tapers dying in the solar ray;
Their forms like wounded earth-worms heavy weigh'd
In th' unaccustom'd effort that they made;
And some fell back to where they lay before;
   Others retain'd the change they had assumed,
And settling darkly in their thoughts of yore,
   To every outer thing their senselessness resumed.

LXI.

A few around us came, dark ghosts and pale,—
   No beam of man or angel in their eye;
And join'd their gaze to him who heard my tale,
   And scann'd me mockingly, I knew not why.
I to their gaze return'd such glance as came
Forth from the kindling soul's excited flame;
For what had they to do with scorn and me?
   Forfeit in them the rights that still were mine;
And they, lost spirits! were no longer free
   To seek the further bourne, where human grows divine.

LXII.

Pity I had for aught so lowly sunk;
   But pity brook'd not from these less than men.
Should they deride the heav'n whence they had shrunk,
   And mock the goal which they had fail'd to gain?
Yet Anger melted, e'en as it had done.
Should madmen seek to touch some saner one;
 He patiently would hear them tell that light
   No longer from the sun pour'd forth its ray;
And having listen'd to their tale of night,
   Go forth and take the sun to guide his onward way.

LXIII.

"Young stranger," said the phantom, "Thou art he
   Who, some have told in my regardless ear,
Art wafted from the realms of earth to be
   A transient dweller in this distant sphere.
Still haunt thine eye those beams, illumed in vain,
Which, once extinguish'd, never light again;
The beams of hope, which only childhood wears,
Quench'd ere our manhood by a thousand tears.
But thou art still upon the verge of life;
   Deceived full oft, but not enough deceived;
And dream'st of days with better fortunes rife,—
   Ay, I too, once, in Hope, the shadow's shade, believed.

LXIV.

"Yon world upon me open'd bright and fair—
   Or seeming fair; and with a painted brow
Smiled on my trusting eye, as free from care,
   And drew the mask before its inward woe.
Urged by the inborn impulse of my soul,
I sprang to joy, and drain'd the offer'd bowl;
And yet that world, e'en while I drank delight,
Dropp'd poison in, the wine of life to blight.
It mimick'd Love, Joy, Friendship's, Beauty's glow,
   Yet scarce the wine was sweet, all gall the lees;
The pleasure madden'd, and the after woe
   Struck in my trusting heat its serpent agonies.

LXV.

"I shared with one my thoughts, my heart, my home
   He was my half of life—my all of joy:
That friend deceived,—ere long I was become
   His fortune's tool—his pleasure's barter'd toy.
I loved a form that shone upon my way,
As 'twere the guardian planet of my day.
I follow'd blindly on the luring beam,
   Nor heeded where it led, nor whom it cross'd
Then when 'twas loveliest, the mocking dream
   Dissolved in air; and with it all was lost.

LXVI.

"Farewell, then, to the world; I cid not leave
   My curse on that scorn'd too much to hate;
But from my heart I loosed the ties that weave
   A chain betwixt it and our human fate.
Bright creatures pass'd me, but I would not love,
Earth's woeful children, but they did not move;
Men hoped and wept, desired, felt, labour'd, thought;
And I stood by and smiled at all they sought.
What had the heart they wrung to do with them?
   It once had answer'd every human cry
But taught by scorn the scorners to contemn,
   I turned my heart's dark side to every mortal eye.

LXVII.

"So lived I—all forgetting—half forgot,—
   Wrapp'd in myself, a world that was mine own;
Nor God nor man had eased my dreary lot,
   And I could teach myself to live alone.
So died I—ay, my dog was couch'd beside,
And lick'd my hand; I felt it as I died.
No human thing then feign'd the grief he felt;
   No eyes shed tears, I had but ill believed;
I went, and left whom Promise still could melt,
To be lured on like me—like me, too, undeceived.

LXVIII.

"I have been lonely—I am lonely still;
   I dug all tenderness from out my heart;
There is no fibre of the smiling ill
   To grow out again, to torture, and depart.

I sit and muse, as I have mused before,
And darker grow the wrongs I ponder o'er.
More cursed the doom of the immortal soul,
More evil all the universal whole.
My powers of mind go forth, and learn despair,
    My powers of heart are dried. What oozes on
Was wont upon a dog to spend its care;
    It fastens now upon this rifted stone."

LXIX.

"Thy griefs are half thine own, mine all of Fate,"
    Another Phantom of the circle cried;
I turn'd, and mark'd him, where deject he sate,
    Contrasted with the former's gloom of pride.
Not altogether so defaced with woe
Was human glory on his pallid brow;
Not so forlorn in self-made solitude,
Banish'd from God and man, appear'd his mood.
It rather seem'd the soul's elastic wing,
    Form'd to grow strong on earth, expand in heaven,
Had suffer'd earthly storms to damp its spring,
    And could not soar at last,—relax'd, decay'd, and riven.

LXX.

"I ask'd not much," he said; and milder flow'd
    His words and tone, as though less sear'd his heart;
"My native land was all I knew of good,
    My joy to dwell, my torture to depart.
The scene, the speech, the visage, which had grown
First on my ear and heart stood there alone;
Colours wherein my mind its forms had weaved,
And tones in which my thoughts were all conceived.
O'er its loved crags and mountains did the air
    Breathe more like life than other air to me;—
The very faults were dear which met me there,—
    They spoke the land of my nativity.

LXXI.

"To wander freely o'er my native hills,
    To talk with others in my native tongue,
To feel in her renown such worth, as steals
    From the land's actions o'er her humblest throng:

This was my boyish joy, my manhood's pride,
Ambition's utmost,—yet was this denied.
Ah! dark in Memory frowns the bitter day,
When from my country I was forced away;
 And still look'd back upon the lessening shore,
    Which seem'd a cloud, a shadow on the sea;
Yet held within its outline, thus obscure,
    The cliffs, the streams, the home, life's life and joy to me.

LXXII.

I came to sunny climes, where Nature's mirth
    And Nature's tenderest softness seemed to twine;
Which they who call'd them theirs, deemed first of Earth—
    I blamed them not, for so to me were mine.
I saw fair scenes; but, ah! they only brought
Remembrance of far dearer to my thought,
Till tears the present image veil'd, and then
Behind their mists the lost land rose again;
That land which smiled, although I saw it not,
    And wore the aspect I had watch'd for years,
Whose mother-image is by none forgot,
    Stamp'd by the joy of youth, burn'd in by manhood'd tears.

LXXIII.

"Then, wretched exile! would I sit me down,
    Where some high point look'd furthest o'er the Sea,
And gaze towards the spot whole hours alone,
    Where home and native land were once for me.
And if the billows inward sent their spray,
And told of breezes winging thence their way,
I bent my knee to feel that wind pass o'er,
Which had been where I fain would be once more;
I sent my sighs on the returning air,
    I spread mine arms toward the viewless shore;
My bosom centred all its yearnings there,
    To Friendship's accents deaf, to Love's best kindness sore.

LXXIV.

"At length, at length,—oh day, whose burst of bliss
    I dream'd not then, and understand not now!—
The word was spoke that ended woe like this,
    The ban was taken from my exiled brow.

A storm raged wild: I thank'd kind Heaven, and gave
My wealth to one to bear me o'er the wave;
And, like a sea-bird, o'er the billow's snow
Sped my wild bark, and yet I deem'd it slow.
Night fell, and all was hidden in its veil,—
    The Morning dawn'd, and port and peak were nigh;
Oh, human strength could little then avail!
    The heart, half broke with woe, now burst at once for joy.

LXXV.

"So died I, gazing on the land I loved,
    By joy's forgotten passion o'er-oppress'd;
It killed the feeble frame through which it moved—
    The soul was grown too pow'rless to be bless'd.
Hope died within it, Pleasure sank subdued,
And Grief alone became its natural mood.
Awhile I wander'd viewless upon Earth,
And grieved while gazing e'en on my home's hearth.
 On mountain ridge and lake's lone shore I sigh'd,
And swept in wailing winds o'er Ocean'd tide;
Until to happier souls awhile 'twas given
To make the land they, too, had loved, their heaven.
Then, from their presence sent, I had my place
    Here, where the wretched of existence dwell;
A land create, perchance, for good and grace,
    But 'tis to me, like all beside, a hell!"

LXXVI.

"Feeble thou wert," another Spectre cried,
    Who wore a female shape, and sate apart,
As though her grief, unmatch'd by aught beside,
    Stood king-like, amid many a broken heart.
"Feeble thou wert; and what except Dismay
Could'st hope when Earth's few years were pass'd away;
And with them borne the clay, the rill, the tree,
Which make up home's best portraiture to thee?
 Home is not there, where flows th' accustom'd tide;
    Not in the vale that breathes a native air;
Not in the hearth that we have lived beside,—
    It is the living forms, who were Companions there.

LXXVII.

"Oh, I had gone wherever snow or sun
   Froze Nature's breast, or cover'd it with flow'rs;
And if meanwhile on mine I bore my son,
   Had thought each scene we pass'd my native bow'rs.
I knew not where more precious breezes blew,
Save as they touch'd his cheek with healthier hue;
I mark'd not where there shone a bluer sky,
Save as reflected from his brighter eye.
There was my mirror of the world without,
   My altar for the world beyond our view;
Through him, and to him pass'd, each social thought,
   And worship of that gift was all the creed I knew.

LXXVIII.

"My Boy, my First-born, my Beatitude,
   Died on this nursing breast, that flow'd in vain;
Pain in those eyes that used to seek me stood,
   The clasping fingers now were stretch'd by pain:
And when they glazed and stiffen'd, what was I?
A Mother, and beheld my first-born die!
Oh! surely then my part on earth was done,
My time pass'd by, my aim and purpose gone.
I, too, must die! and from that hour unblest,
   Food I refused, and starved the vital flame.
Could I have borne to feel it fill my breast,
   And have no cherub lip to drink it when it came?

LXXIX.

"They spoke of comfort, but I closed the ear
   That used to listen to my Infant's strain;
That voice was gone, and ne'er should one less dear,
   With baser sounds, the Mother's ear profane.
They fain would join my hands and lift my eyes,
In prayer submissive, toward the angry skies;
But, no! He gave the treasure that was gone;
He bound my soul about that taken one;
And I, obedient more to Nature's call,
Clasp'd my cold boy, and wept upon his pall.
I, too, was ready, since his time was done;
   And when full soon upon him closed the tomb,
True to the thoughts which through my life had run,
   I died upon his grave, whose birth-place was my womb."

LXXX.

Thus spake, thus paused they, and with frame oppress'd,
  Languid or rigid, like their several pain,
Each, when his tale of sorrow was express'd,
  Sank back to gloominess or grief again.
I mark'd them as on earth we sometimes stand
Before the tomb-place of an ancient land,
 Within whose bourne, in desolation drear,
  Name, Nation, Story, with the dust are laid:
But Hope descends to dry for them the tear—
  These had left Hope behind—they were the risen dead.

LXXXI.

Oh! had they thought, while yet 'twas time to think,
  How Grief to human souls is like the breeze,
Which wafts the bark, that lengthen'd calms would sink,
  In triumph home across the conquer'd seas!
Had they but raised their thoughts so high as man
Has power to look beyond his mortal span;
And o'er their human misery watch'd the star
  Of their great fortunes in the upper sky!
Victorious urged o'er mortal griefs the war,
  And in the strife confirm'd their nature's dignity.

LXXXII.

For 'tis not only in the sun to bask,
  Nor by bright hearths to shun the tempest's rage,
That man is summon'd to his earthly task,
  And shewn afar his native heritage.
More glorious labours are assign'd the race
Whose future home is all the breadth of space,
And who in many a fight must win the strength
Which nerves their spirits to that height at length;
E'en as the Falcon, when the wind is fair,
  Close to the earth on lagging pinions goes,
But when against her beats the adverse air,
  She breasts the gale, and rises as it blows.

END OF CANTO I. (THE AMBITION OF FURTHER CANTOS WAS NEVER REALISED)